BUMPIN' UGLIES

Episode 3 – Scratch and Sniff

Brandon Wilkinson
and
S.E. Miller

By the same author

- Memoirs of the Messed Up Minds
- Me 1 Arthritis 0
- Beer Goggles
- The Tin Boy
- Dirty Dealer
- Bumpin' Uglies
    - Episode 1 – A Pain in the Ass
    - Episode 2 – Date with The Prostate

Introduction

The Bumpin' Uglies series is a work of fiction very loosely based on the Central Florida complex named The Villages, the largest gated retirement community in the United States. Over the years it gained the reputation of being quite the party place, stories emerging of sex, sensuality, and general shenanigans.

Around 2006 a Villages gynecologist rather controversially stated in an interview that she'd treated more cases of herpes and human papillomavirus at The Villages than she had during the time she'd practiced in Miami.

These types of reports tickled our creativity and Bumpin' Uglies was born.

Scratch and Sniff is Episode 3 of 8 of the Bumpin' Uglies series, written in an entertaining script format by creators Brandon Wilkinson and S.E. Miller.

INT. MARSHALL'S APARTMENT. NIGHT

We see Marshall sat on his couch, blanket covering his lap. One hand is under the blanket moving rhythmically up and down, his other hand is holding his cellphone to his ear.

MARSHALL

So, Vicky, how long have you been using the chat line then?

VICKY

A few months, Marshall. I've met a lot of interesting people on here.

MARSHALL

Nice. So you actually meet the people you chat to?

VICKY

Not very often. Depends if I really vibe with them and whether they live nearby. Where are you located?

MARSHALL

Florida. What about you?

VICKY

Tampa.

MARSHALL

Really?

VICKY

Nah, just fucking with you. I'm in Houston, Texas.

MARSHALL

I was going to say that would've been quite the coincidence. How old are you?

VICKY

Twenty-eight. You?

MARSHALL

Got you by ten years. I'm thirty-eight.

VICKY

Nice, I like myself an older man. Love the maturity and life experience.

MARSHALL

Well there you go. I've certainly got some years on you and I've got plenty of life experience.

VICKY

That's hot. I love your name. Were you named after Marshall Mathers?

Marshall remains silent.

You know, Marshall Mathers…Eminem…the rapper.

MARSHALL

Oh...yes...I mean no. Not named after him, but he is a favorite of mine.

The blank look on his face is priceless.

                    VICKY
Awesome. So what do you like to do for fun, Marshall? Do you like to get naughty?

                    MARSHALL
Me? Yes. Naughty is my middle name. Do *you* like to get naughty?

                    VICKY
That's why I'm on here Marshall. I want to get naughty right now. I love your voice. You've already made my panties wet. Would you like to talk dirty and masturbate with me for a while?

Marshall's hand rhythm under the blanket intensifies.

                    MARSHALL
Let's do it. Just hope our definitions of a while aren't wildly different. What are you wearing?

                    VICKY
Just these red panties and nothing else. I'm soaked. Are you hard?

                    MARSHALL
Yep, I could hit a home run with this bat right now.

                              VICKY

Marshall, you are naughty. I'm just picturing that big
bat right now and I'm getting a little sweaty.

                            MARSHALL

Well, it is pretty big.

                              VICKY

How big are you Marshall?

                            MARSHALL

I'm just kidding. I'm not that big at all. I think I am
maybe a little over eight inches.

                              VICKY

That's huge Marshall. You'll need to make do with
my pussy then. No way that monster is getting
anywhere near my butthole.

A frenzy is occurring under Marshall's blanket.

                            MARSHALL

Are you touching yourself?

                              VICKY

I have been for a few minutes now. What do you
want to do to me?

                            MARSHALL

I want to touch your boobies. Squeeze those dirty love pillows.

VICKY
Interesting choice and interesting word selection, but go on.

MARSHALL
I want to motorboat those big bouncing balloons and rub those moist panties.

VICKY
O...K. Let's focus on the panties Marshall. I love that. Do you like wet panties?

MARSHALL
Love them.

VICKY
Would you like me to send you this wet pair I have on right now?

MARSHALL
Oh my God, oh my God, oh my God. Aaaaaaaahhhhhh.

The hand antics under the blanket come to an abrupt halt.

VICKY
Did you just cum?

                    MARSHALL
Yes, sorry.

                    VICKY
Don't be sorry, Marshall. Happy I could get you off or
at least help get you off. On a serious note, would
you like to have this wet thong?

                    MARSHALL
Does the Tin Man have a sheet metal cock?

                    VICKY
Huh?

                    MARSHALL
Yes, yes I would.

                    VICKY
I sell my used panties for a living.

                    MARSHALL
You sell them?

                    VICKY
Yes, they're for sale.

                    MARSHALL
How much?

                    VICKY

Forty dollars.

                        MARSHALL
For one pair?

                          VICKY
Yes, but I do two for seventy or three for ninety.

                        MARSHALL
You mail them?

                          VICKY
Well I'm not going to drive them there.

                        MARSHALL
Sorry, that was a dumb question. Won't they be dry
by the time I receive them in the mail?

                          VICKY
Nope. I wear them for a day, masturbate twice in
them, throw in a workout, then I vacuum pack them.
When you receive and cut open the vacuum pack, it's
like you just took them directly off my body. From
there you can sniff them, wrap them around your
penis, or do whatever the hell you want with them.

                        MARSHALL
Holy shit. I'll take the pair you have on now. Let me
start with just the one.

                          VICKY

You'll need to go on my website and order them. Check it out. They'll be on there in about twenty minutes. They are red with a white heart on the front. My site is Victoria wet panty secret dot com. All one word.

MARSHALL

I'm on it.

EXT. APARTMENT COMPLEX POOL. MORNING

Jack and Diego sit at an umbrella covered table by the pool sipping on coffee. A large white dog is snuggled in next to Jack's feet. Diego is perched on what seems to be an enormous ice pack. Marshall appears with a package under his arm.

MARSHALL

Morning cock gobblers.

JACK

Ah, good morning my little virgin friend, and why are you looking so happy with yourself today? Did you happen to find your dick on the first attempt this morning?

MARSHALL

Don't be ridiculous, that'll never happen. No, a package arrived this morning and I wanted to open it with you both. What the hell is that?

JACK

This is Tyson. My daughter and family are off to
Mexico for a couple of weeks so I said I would take
him rather than having him go to the kennel.

MARSHALL

Why on earth would you do that?

JACK

For one, he's a great dog. American Bulldog. Nobody
in their right mind would fuck with you with him by
your side. Secondly, he's a pussy magnet. Every time
I walk him the women come over to me for a stroke.
I mean a stroke of the dog Marshall, before your
mind gets all carried away.

MARSHALL

Can I take him for a walk later and test out that
statement?

JACK

Not a chance. He's one hundred and twenty-five
pounds of solid muscle. He'd be the one walking you.
I will say this though, facially you both look
remarkably similar. You could be twins.

MARSHALL

Diego, what the hell are you sitting on?

DIEGO

Ice pack.

                    MARSHALL
Why?

                      JACK
His asshole is still throbbing since its encounter with
Dr. Frankfurter Fingers.

*Marshall and Jack howl with laughter. Diego returns
a scowl.*

                    MARSHALL
That's hilarious.

                     DIEGO
Yeah, priceless! Feel like I've been raped with a
fucking frozen pineapple.

                    MARSHALL
Could be worse.

                     DIEGO
How?

                    MARSHALL
You could've *actually* been raped by someone
shoving a frozen pineapple in and out of your dried
up little asshole.

They all explode with laughter this time.

DIEGO

I guess so. Never again unless I get that little Asian
woman you got for your prostate exam. Anyway,
enough chat about my pulsating pooper. Sit down
and show us this thing you got delivered.

*Marshall sits. Tyson remains asleep. The small
package is opened to reveal a pair of red knickers in a
clear vacuum pack.*

MARSHALL

Ta-da.

JACK

You bought yourself a pair of fucking panties?

MARSHALL

Not any old pair of panties. Used panties.

DIEGO

Used? Like second hand?

MARSHALL

Well...yes...but with a twist. I've been on this chat
line at night a couple of times a week. It's basically
just people who want to talk dirty and jerk off. It's
great, they can't see you so you can pretend to be
whoever you want to be.

JACK

Let me guess, you're a young, successful, good looking, and well hung man while you're on there?

Marshall clears his throat.

                    MARSHALL
Anyway...a few nights ago I was jerking off with this twenty-eight year-old on the other end of the phone.. She said her knickers were really wet. *These* are those very panties.

                    DIEGO
She sent you her dirty panties?

                    MARSHALL
Technically yes, but with a slight spin. I bought them. That's what she does for a living. Sells her dirty underwear. Each pair she sells she says she wears for the day, has a workout in them, and paddles the pink canoe twice with them on.

                    DIEGO
There is no way she said she paddles her pink canoe. Where do you get this shit?

                    MARSHALL
OK, low-fives herself twice a day while wearing them.

                    JACK

Fuck off Marshall. Paddling the pink canoe was more convincing. What woman gives herself five fingers down there? Two or three would seem way more convincing. Five would be your equivalent of needing to use both hands.

                    MARSHALL
Right, she masturbates twice with them on. For fuck's sake. Can't even add a little entertainment to a story.

                    DIEGO
So the contents of that bag contain her vajizzle-covered knickers.

                    MARSHALL
You've got to be fucking kidding me. I get a hard time for paddling her pink canoe and you just use vajizzle to describe female sex emissions.

                    JACK
He does make a valid point my friend, but I do love the word vajizzle.

Jack and Diego share a high-five.

                    MARSHALL
So yes, this bag contains knickers doused with her lady spray.

                    DIEGO

Lady spray?

Now they are all in stitches.

MARSHALL
Here's one for you, Jack. They are smothered with
her 'E-Jack-ulate.'

JACK
Shouldn't it be 'E-Jill-ulate'?

Their hilarity ensues.

MARSHALL
Right, timeout. Yes, basically they are covered in her
cum and sweat and whatever else.

JACK
That's actually pretty gross. Anyway, get it open and
give us a sniff.

*The three again erupt with laughter. Marshall rips
open the bag, carefully removes the panties, and
holds them out. All three tentatively move in for a
smell.*

DIEGO
Jesus Christ, that's pungent. It's like a pee and pussy
cocktail.

MARSHALL

They're still wet; I can feel it on my fingers.

DIEGO

It's sort of gross, but that hint of sex makes me want another go.

They all venture back in for another inhale. Tyson awakens, raises his head and sniffs the air.

JACK

How much did you pay?

MARSHALL

Forty dollars plus shipping?

JACK

What?

MARSHALL

Expensive, right?

JACK

Very much so. A nice little earner for her. How do you know she was twenty-eight and not fifty-eight?

MARSHALL

Don't know, don't care. Anyway, I'll catch you guys at the clubhouse tonight. Heading home to wear these nasty knickers like a face mask while enjoying some Beef Strokenoff.

                    DIEGO

For fuck's sake. Here we go again with the
euphemisms.

INT. CLUBHOUSE. NIGHT

*Jack and Diego enter the clubhouse. There is a light
scattering of residents, but very few women to speak
of. Marshall sits alone at their regular table by the
bar.*

                    JACK

Well, well, look who's here already. Surprised you
managed to drag yourself away from your new
cotton girlfriend.

                    MARSHALL

Satin.

                    JACK

My bad. Hope you gave your face a wash before
coming out.

                    MARSHALL

I did...reluctantly. I can still smell her though. Think
her taco juice has melded with my nose hairs.

                    DIEGO

Barf. You've probably got them with you. Are they
your new handkerchief?

MARSHALL

Don't be so ridiculous.

JACK

You don't have them with you?

MARSHALL

OK, yes I do, but just in case of emergency.

DIEGO

Emergency? What sort of emergency is going to require a pair of old funky knickers to take care of? I guess if someone passes out and there is a shortage of smelling salts to revive.

MARSHALL

Shut up Diego. You know I sometimes have issues getting an erection. What if I score tonight? I might need a quick sniff of them to get my dick in the game.

JACK

Marshall, there's more chance of Stephen Hawking successfully completing every page of the Kama Sutra on a Friday evening than you having one of our old crusties here attempting to tease your little maggot out those shorts.

MARSHALL

Because he's dead now?

                    JACK
Yeah, Marshall, that was the joke.

*Jack and Diego sit down and Pam brings them a
drink.*

                  MARSHALL
Listen, I was thinking.

                   DIEGO
This could be dangerous.

                  MARSHALL
For once I am being serious, so please hear me out.

                    JACK
Go ahead.

                  MARSHALL
This girl Vicky, or whatever her real name was. The
one who sold me the panties. Let's say she actually
only wears them half a day. So, two pairs per day,
and let's assume a thirty day month. That's sixty
pairs per month potentially, at forty bucks a pop.
That's two thousand four hundred dollars per month
for a one person operation.

                    JACK
Someone's had their calculator out to play.

MARSHALL
Well of course I did. One of the many reasons I look
at breasts is to help me count to two.

DIEGO
What are you getting at Marshall?

MARSHALL
We're always talking about money making schemes.
Let's get in on this shit. Jack, you know all about this
website and internet stuff. You could have a website
put together. We buy a vacuum pack machine. We
can get a cheap one of those for a couple of
hundred. We put an ad out in the local rag and
recruit, say, three girls. That would give us
potentially seven thousand two hundred bucks per
month. Half goes to the girls and we take the other
half. Split three ways with us and that's twelve
hundred a piece.

JACK
You know something Marshall, this might actually be
the only decent idea you've ever come up with.

MARSHALL
I'll take that as a compliment.

DIEGO
You think it's a viable idea Jack?

JACK

Actually I do. The website part is a piece of piss. I could knock that out in an afternoon. Expense there would be less than fifteen bucks per month. The hardest part will be recruitment.

                    DIEGO
Could we not just grab a few of the old gals here?

                    MARSHALL
Fuck off.

                    JACK
Come on Diego. Pussy is like a carton of milk, not a bottle of fine wine. It isn't getting better as time goes by. No, we want the scent of succulent young snatch. Anyway, there's a reason the term granny panties came into existence. The ass size of the ones we typically tap are not exactly what the used underwear market is looking for. No we need age forties or less and ones in decent shape.

                    MARSHALL
What should we put in the newspaper ad?

                    DIEGO
Right, I don't think we can just go all out and put in an ad that we want their used underwear.

                    JACK

Let's just post an ad looking for females for adult entertainment and leave it at that. We get say three we want to talk with and face-to-face we explain the deal. The sweet thing for them is that they don't really need to do shit. Fuck, they could even do a regular job while they work for us. All they are doing is walking around grinding their bits around on the panties, sneaking in a little finger action when they can. On a daily basis one of us makes a run to collect the panties, we take a few pics of them, post those on the website, vacuum pack them, and then wait for the orders to flood in. We'll need to advertise on a few places like Craigslist or the likes and maybe local porn shops, but shouldn't be a major issue. There are dirty buggers everywhere. Shit, half the old fuckers in our apartment complex will be on this like a rash.

DIEGO
This is beginning to sound good.

MARSHALL
See, I'm not just a pretty face.

JACK
That's hilarious Marshall. I'll get working on the ad.

INT. PANCAKE PLACE RESTAURANT. MORNING

Jack, Diego, and Marshall occupy a booth in the far corner. Jack is on the side facing the restaurant entrance, Diego and Marshall on the other side. They all have coffee in front of them and Diego and Marshall have pads and pens perched on the table.

DIEGO
So we are interviewing three women?

JACK
Correct. Spoke to them and they all seemed keen to chat. I was a little sparse on the details, but let me do the talking. You guys take some notes. I doubt we'll need them but it just adds a little professionalism in my mind.

MARSHALL
What should I write down? Tit size and stuff like that?

JACK
What the hell does tit size have to do with wearing panties?

MARSHALL
OK, butt size.

JACK

Slightly more relevant, but I was thinking more marks out of ten for enthusiasm. We want workers into this idea. Those who are going to take it seriously and be eager to get us the used goods and make us all a lot of cash.

                    MARSHALL
Got it.

A woman enters the establishment and the Jack takes note. She is looking around like she is trying to find someone. Jack waves and catches her attention. She has dark hair tied back in a ponytail and looks in her mid-thirties. She is dressed in a vest top, Lycra shorts, and looks like she just got done working out. Jack stands up as she approaches.

                    JACK
Are you Melanie?

                    LADY
Yes, are you Jack?

                    JACK
Yes I am. Take a seat.

Jack squeezes in beside Diego and Marshall.

                    MELANIE
Nice to meet you Jack.

JACK

These are my business partners, Diego and Marshall.

MELANIE

Nice to meet you both.

JACK

Are we a little older than you were expecting?

MELANIE

Yes, but that's OK. Sorry, I didn't mean to offend.

JACK

In our business there is no offence.

MELANIE

And what is this business? It wasn't clear.

JACK

Underwear modeling you could say.

MELANIE

Underwear?

JACK

Used underwear.

MELANIE

Not porn?

JACK

You were hoping it was porn?

MELANIE

Not hoping. I've done that before though. Just when the ad said adult entertainment, I guess I assumed.

MARSHALL

You've done porn before?

JACK

Marshall, enough please. Yes, the underwear business. We sell used underwear. We recruit good looking women like yourself and sell your used goods. We supply the underwear, you wear it for half a day, get sweaty, perhaps masturbate, we take them from you and sell them on. You receive fifty percent. We sell for forty bucks and you get twenty for each pair we get from you. Money up front.

MELANIE

Interesting. All I need to do is wear them, get my fluids on them and give them back to you and I get cash?

JACK

Precisely.

MELANIE

So it wouldn't even have to interfere with my current job?

                    JACK

Not in the slightest.

                  MELANIE

Sounds like a win win.

                    JACK

What is it you do right now?

                  MELANIE

I run fitness classes at the local gym. Just came from
there.

                    JACK

Wearing panties now?

                  MELANIE

Umm...yes.

                    JACK

Those are probably good to go then for a first
sample.

                  MELANIE

Thought you said you supplied the panties?

                    JACK

Are you pretty attached to those ones?

                  MELANIE

Well, I was sweating during the workout quite a bit, so they are stuck to me pretty good.

                    JACK
I meant any emotional attachment.

                    MELANIE
Hahaha, I see. No, I never wear my best to morning class. They are decent though. They got drenched in the workout.

                    JACK
Don't suppose you masturbated in them before class?

                    MELANIE
Nope, but I can take care of that now if you'd like?

Marshall and Diego's mouths hang open.

                    JACK
Right here?

                    MELANIE
Well, I was thinking about popping to the ladies room, but I'm down doing it here if you'd like to watch. You'd just need to keep an eye out for anyone catching me.

                    JACK
You serious?

MELANIE

I love the rush. I'm a bit of an exhibitionist. The thrill of getting caught and all that. Gets me going.

JACK

Whatever works for you.

Melanie looks around. Nobody is close. She slips her hand down the front of her black Lycra shorts and begins. Her eyes close. The guys are speechless. Within no more than a minute she lets out a huge groan.

MELANIE

I just came.

MARSHALL

Me too.

MELANIE

Let me pop to the ladies and I'll bring the panties back to you. Do I have the job?

JACK

I think we both know the answer to that.

INT. PANCAKE PLACE RESTAURANT. 10:30 am

DIEGO

Well...I can hardly believe what just happened, but in light of what we're trying to achieve I would say extremely successful.

JACK

Above and beyond I would say. Did you really blow a load in your pants Marshall?

MARSHALL

No.

JACK

Marshall?

MARSHALL

Of course I did. You didn't?

JACK

I was turned on but I have a little more control than that. You're the only one dumping your beans in your briefs, right Diego?

Diego's head drops.

Oh for fuck's sake the pair of you.

DIEGO

You have to admit, that was intense. It was like being on a porn set.

JACK
I'm glad you both didn't ask me what the dress code should be for today's interviews.

MARSHALL
Not following.

DIEGO
Me neither.

JACK
Well I would've probably told you both to just come in your pants.

Jack goes into fits of laughter.

MARSHALL
Piss off, Jack. Right who's next?

JACK
A woman by the name of Jackie. Good name. I like. Sexy voice. Husky.

DIEGO
Well let's hope she's as enthusiastic as the last little sexpot.

MARSHALL

I hope not. My ticker might not survive it.

                    JACK
Just keep your hands above the table at all times.

                    DIEGO
Does that apply to me also?

                    JACK
It applies to all three of us my friend.

A redheaded woman enters the establishment looking around vacantly. She's late-forties, more fat on a butcher's apron than her entire sculpted body, gorgeous flowing long hair, but a face on her like a grieving pug. Jack sends a wave and she looks relieved.

                    REDHEAD
Are you Jack?

Jack stands and holds out his hand.

                    JACK
That would be me.

                    REDHEAD
Hi Jack, I'm Jackie.

                    MARSHALL
Don't be saying that at the airport.

Marshall erupts with laughter, but he's on his own.

                    JACKIE
Excuse me?

                    JACK
Jackie, this is one of my colleagues, Marshall. This is
Diego. Apologies, I have no idea what he is talking
about. What are you talking about?

                    MARSHALL
Hi Jack. Hijack. Forget it. I'm nervous, leave me
alone.

                    JACK
Take a seat Jackie.

                    JACKIE
So, exactly what sort of adult entertainment work
am I interviewing for?

                    JACK
Let me pose a question to you. What do you think
the role is?

                    JACKIE

If I was guessing I would say some sort of fetish internet porn, probably old man or men with younger women stuff. I am assuming it would be having sex on camera with you guys for the online site you run. Just so you know, I am fine with that. Age is just a number to me.

MARSHALL
You are absolutely dead on. Can you start now?

JACK
Shut up Marshall. Jackie, it is adult entertainment of a sort, but there is no need for any nudity, and certainly no requirement for any frolicking with the likes of us three.

MARSHALL
No requirement, but...

JACK
Marshall, shut your pie hole.

JACKIE
You certainly are a frisky one, Marshall.

JACK
He's going to be a frisky one with a bruised pair of balls in about two minutes.

MARSHALL

Well they are already a little swollen. Know what I'm saying Jackie?

                    DIEGO
Dear Lord.

*Jackie is all smiles and seems genuinely entertained
with the banter.*

                    JACK
Let's get back to the real matter at hand, and I'll get
straight to the point before my little troll of a friend
has his next outburst. We want your used
underwear. Well, we'll provide the panties, you wear
them for half a day, get them wet, get your scent on
them, we pick them up from you and we sell them
online. There is quite the fetish market out there.

                    JACKIE
Interesting.

                    JACK
Thoughts?

                    JACKIE
And by wet you mean I should masturbate while
wearing them?

                    JACK
Ideally yes. Would that be a problem?

Jackie laughs loudly enough that a few patrons at distant booths turnaround.

                    JACKIE
I do it regularly so no issue. At least twice per day. First thing before I get out of bed and last thing before I go to sleep. On my days off work it could be a lot more.

Marshall and Diego both take out handkerchiefs and start mopping their foreheads.

                    JACK
What do you do for a living Jackie?

                    JACKIE
I'm a massage therapist.

                    MARSHALL
A proper one or are you in the happy ending trade?

                    JACK
Would you please stop?

                    JACKIE
It's fine Jack. Marshall, if you are asking if I jerk my clients off towards the end of their session, then no. I am an extremely sexual person, but I do take my job seriously and I'm professional at all times.

                    MARSHALL

Bummer.

JACKIE
You're a little sexually frustrated aren't you Marshall?

MARSHALL
Without question.

JACK
Stop feeling sorry for him Jackie. So, what do you think? Our expectations would be one or two pairs per day, we sell each for forty dollars, you get twenty per pair, and we pay you on the spot for each one we receive.

JACKIE
I'm in. Easy money it seems. I won't let you down.

JACK
Great, you're hired.

MARSHALL
Can I book an appointment for a massage? Not looking for anything sexual. Just got a lot of aches and pains.

JACKIE
Of course. Let me give you my card. What pain are you experiencing?

MARSHALL

I think I might've pulled a muscle in my cock.

JACK

I'll be in touch Jackie. Now please excuse me while I slap the shit out of my friend.

A waitress arrives with another pot of coffee.

JACK

Marshall, for fuck's sake, please keep your shit together.

MARSHALL

It's hard when we're talking to these younger women with hot bodies.

JACK

Look, I know it's difficult.

MARSHALL

No Jack, it's hard, literally hard. I'm pitching a fucking undie tent at the moment and I forgot to take the Cialis this morning.

JACK

Look, keep your cool. I'm tingling also, but this is business. How are you doing Diego?

DIEGO

Feeling a little lightheaded. I think most of the blood
has found its way to my Cuban cigar.

                          JACK
Hang in there, just one more to go.

                        MARSHALL
Who now?

                          JACK
Woman by the name of Nanette.

                         DIEGO
Nanette?

                          JACK
Yes, a little different. High-pitched voice, probably
young. Sounded super enthusiastic though.

                        MARSHALL
How young do you think? If a teenager comes
through that door I am out of here. No way will I be
part of some pedophile sting.

                          JACK
Me neither. If she looks super young I will be asking
for identification before proceeding.

                         DIEGO
Fuck. Don't look now, but Yo-Yo Knickers just walked
in the front door.

JACK

Shit. Stay quiet and keep your heads down.

Yo-Yo Knickers proceeds to walk towards them.

JACK

Hi Nancy, how are you? In for some breakfast?

YO-YO KNICKERS

Hi boys. No, have an interview for a job.

Jack sighs.

JACK

You're Nanette, aren't you?

YO-YO KNICKERS

That would be correct. You know, I wasn't certain it was you on the phone when we spoke as it always sounds a little different than in person, but I had my suspicions.

JACK

Then why did you try and disguise your voice with that high-pitched nonsense?

YO-YO KNICKERS

Would we be chatting now if I'd identified myself?

JACK

Absolutely not.

YO-YO KNICKERS
Precisely. Now, what is the adult entertainment job all about?

DIEGO
Nancy, I think you're wasting everyone's time here.

YO-YO KNICKERS
And why on earth would that be? If this is some sort of pornography deal then I'd be an absolute asset. I might be pushing seventy, but I think you'll agree I look significantly younger. Also, I have a very particular set of skills, skills I have acquired over a very long career.

JACK
OK Liam Neeson.

YO-YO KNICKERS
Well I do. Young men still flirt with me. In fact, about six months ago this fella in his early-forties told me as we lay sweating that he believed I could probably suck a tomato through a tennis racket.

MARSHALL
That's a disturbing visual even for me. Although, Jack, I'm getting movement again.

JACK

Nancy, it isn't porn. It's the used underwear business. We are looking for candidates to dirty up their knickers with their scent, we take them and sell them to that particular fetish market.

YO-YO KNICKERS

Perfect, I'm in. I can get my juices flowing on them. I'm the ideal candidate. I'm not like the others in our community who are likely as dry as a nun's gusset down there. Nope I'm still Niagara Falls during arousal.

DIEGO

Feeling movement as well Jack. She's putting forward a pretty compelling case.

JACK

Nancy, this is for sexy underwear. We're not venturing into the granny panties market.

YO-YO KNICKERS

I would bloody well hope not. I'll have you know I'm sporting a silky black G-string at the moment. I can floss my ass crack with it without even getting out of them.

MARSHALL

No shit!

YO-YO KNICKERS

Very rarely.

                              JACK
For fuck's sake.

                         YO-YO KNICKERS
So am I hired? Raise your hand if you want me on the
team.

*Jack shakes his head and turns to Diego and
Marshall. Both their arms are vertical, fingers
pointing to the ceiling.*

                              JACK
Well…looks like you're in. Majority rules.

INT. CLUBHOUSE. EVENING

*It's a quiet night at the clubhouse. The boys are
perched at their usual table, Pam the bartender sits
with them as there are no other drinks to pour. Jack
has his daughter's dog, Tyson, snuggled in by his feet,
twitching, dreaming of chasing rabbits or munching
down sausages.*

                              JACK

OK, it's been two weeks to this day since we started this venture. All three of our employees have regimentally given us two used garments per day. That's eighty-four pairs at twenty bucks a piece we've given out. I've done the calculations already. That's a little shy of seventeen-hundred dollars. We've sold four pairs! We are sitting on an inventory nightmare. We're losing our asses. A new business model is required and fast.

DIEGO
What are you suggesting, Jack?

JACK
We fire all the girls or at least tell them we are suspending business until further notice. We need to clear some inventory. You know, I've just had an idea. No, they're all fired.

MARSHALL
So we're shutting shop completely?

JACK
Not exactly. Now, gather round and listen.

EXT. LOCAL PARK. DAY

We see the backs of Jack, Diego, and Marshall as they stroll through the park. The camera pans down. They are each wearing shorts with lacy G-strings sticking out above their waistlines. The camera pans down further. Tyson is on leash and is walking rather awkwardly in a pair of bright red female panties.

THE END – Episode 3

www.ingramcontent.com/pod-product-compliance
Lightning Source LLC
Chambersburg PA
CBHW020516160726
47991CB00007B/2977